DISCOVERING
FRANCE

By Jo Sturges

CRESTWOOD HOUSE
New York

A ZOË BOOK

© 1993 Zoë Books Limited

First American publication 1993 by Crestwood House, Macmillan Publishing Company, 866 Third Avenue, New York, NY 10022

Macmillan Publishing Company is part of the Maxwell Communication Group of Companies.

First published in Great Britain in 1993 by Zoë Books Limited, 15 Worthy Lane, Winchester, Hampshire SO23 7AB

Devised and produced by
Zoë Books Limited
15 Worthy Lane
Winchester
Hampshire SO23 7AB

Printed in Italy by Grafedit SpA
Design: Jan Sterling, Sterling Associates
Picture research: Suzanne Williams
Map: Gecko Limited
Production: Grahame Griffiths

8 7 6 5 4 3 2 1

Library of Congress Cataloging-in-Publication Data

Sturges, Jo.
  France / by Jo Sturges.
    p. cm. — (Discovering)
  Summary: Introduces the notable sights, people, culture, and history of France.
  ISBN 0-89686-778-1
  1. France — Juvenile literature. [1. France.]
I. Title. II. Title: Discovering France. III. Series.
DC33.7.S78 1993
944 — dc20   92-35182

Photographic acknowledgments

The publishers wish to acknowledge, with thanks, the following photographic sources:

Cover and title page:Robert Harding Picture Library;5l Zefa;5r © Documentation Française/Didier Le Scour; 6 Robert Harding Picture Library;7l Robert Harding Picture Library/Nigel Blythe;7r Oxford Scientific Films/Okapia/Reic Dragesco;8 Robert Harding Picture Library;9l Zefa;9r Robert Harding Picture Library;10 Zefa;11l Robert Harding Picture Library; 11r © Documentation Française/Thibaut Cuisset;12 © Documentation Française/Almasy; 13l © SODEL-EDF/ Documentation Française/Michel Brigaud;13r Frank Spooner Pictures/Gilles Saussier;14 Robert Harding Picture Library;15l,15r,16 Zefa;17l © SNCF/ Documentation Française/M Henri;17r Rex Features;18 Robert Harding Picture Library; 19l Zefa;19r,20,21l Robert Harding Picture Library;21r Rex Features;22 Zefa;23l Frank Spooner Pictures/Gamma;23r © Documentation Française/Taulin-Hommell;24 Allsport/ Vandystadt/Yahh Guichaoua;25l Claude Monet, *Parliament with the sun breaking through the fog*, Louvre, Paris, Giraudon/ Bridgeman Art Library;25r Rex Features; 26,27l Robert Harding Picture Library; 27r Bridgeman Art Library/Musée Carnavalet, Paris;28 Archives Documentation Française;29l © Documentation Française;29r Robert Harding Picture Library.

Cover: *The Eiffel Tower, Paris, at night*

Title page: *The village of Beynac-et-Cazenac, in the Dordogne*

Contents

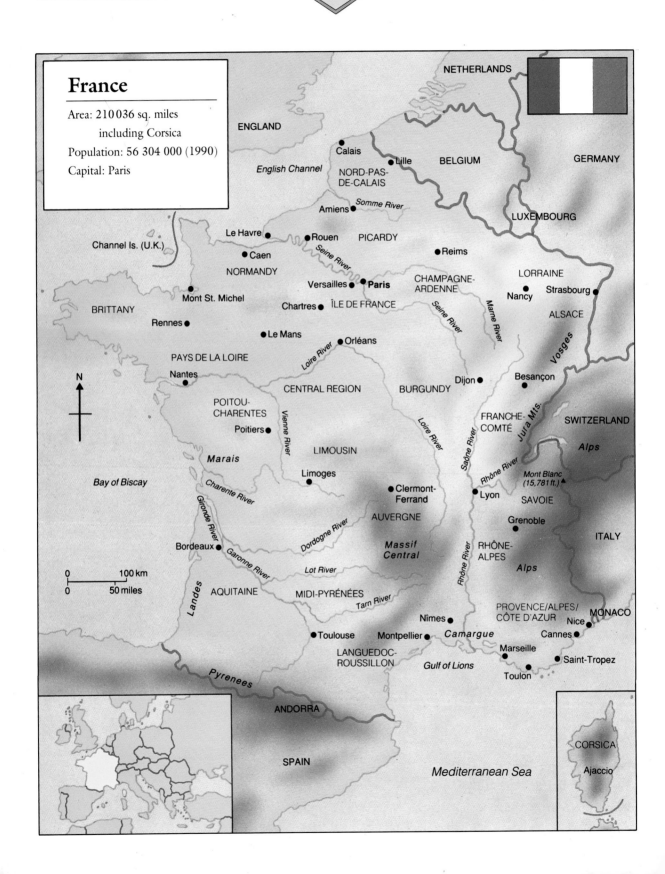

France

Area: 210 036 sq. miles
including Corsica
Population: 56 304 000 (1990)
Capital: Paris

NETHERLANDS

ENGLAND

English Channel

Calais
Lille
BELGIUM

GERMANY

NORD-PAS-
DE-CALAIS

Somme River
Amiens

LUXEMBOURG

Le Havre
Rouen
PICARDY

Reims

LORRAINE

Channel Is. (U.K.)

Caen

NORMANDY

Seine River

Versailles Paris

CHAMPAGNE-
ARDENNE

Nancy

Strasbourg

BRITTANY

Mont St. Michel

Chartres ÎLE DE FRANCE

Seine River

Marne River

ALSACE

Rennes

Le Mans

Orléans
Loire River

Dijon

Besançon

Vosges

PAYS DE LA LOIRE

Nantes

N

CENTRAL REGION

BURGUNDY

FRANCHE-
COMTÉ

SWITZERLAND

POITOU-
CHARENTES

Vienne River

Poitiers

LIMOUSIN

Loire River

Saône River

Jura Mts.

Alps

Marais

Bay of Biscay

Charente River

Limoges

Clermont-
Ferrand

Rhône River

Mont Blanc
(15,781 ft.)

Lyon

SAVOIE

0   100 km
0   50 miles

Gironde River

Bordeaux

Garonne River

Dordogne River

AUVERGNE

Massif
Central

Grenoble

ITALY

Lot River

RHÔNE-
ALPES

Alps

Landes

AQUITAINE

MIDI-PYRÉNÉES

Tarn River

Rhône River

PROVENCE/ALPES/
CÔTE D'AZUR

Nice

MONACO

Nîmes

Camargue

Cannes

Toulouse

Montpellier

Marseille

Saint-Tropez

LANGUEDOC-
ROUSSILLON

Gulf of Lions

Toulon

Pyrenees

ANDORRA

SPAIN

Mediterranean Sea

CORSICA

Ajaccio

Bienvenue!

In central France, fast rivers have cut deep gorges.

Welcome to France, the largest country in Western Europe. On the map France has an almost square shape. It has borders with seven other countries and with three seas. The landscape varies from snow-covered mountain ranges to long, sandy beaches that bake in the summer sun. Narrow gorges with rushing rivers, ancient forests and marshlands are homes to a wonderful variety of plants and wild animals. There are fertile, rolling plains given over to farming. These produce the food and wine for which France has become world famous.

Town and country

France has a long, rich history. Over hundreds of years the country has produced great artists, scientists and thinkers. Visitors will see many fine buildings, such as the magnificent cathedrals of Chartres and Reims. France was involved in many wars in the Middle Ages, so there are many strong castles and old walled cities such as Carcassonne. There are splendid palaces and stately homes called *châteaux*, built to show off the country's wealth. More simple buildings may be seen in the country and on farms. In many cities there are elegant town houses.

Futuroscope

Step into the future! This high-tech college and theme park is near Poitiers. Space-age buildings, such as the crystal-like Kinemax theater, shown below, tower above the countryside. France is famous for its exciting modern architecture.

Mountains and *maquis*

France's landscape includes three mountain regions, three highland regions and three lowland plains, as well as a long and varied coastline.

Most of France has cool summers and mild winters with good rainfall. However, the far south has hot, dry summers and warm winters. The mountain regions also have hot summers but have cold winters with plenty of snow.

Large areas of France are covered in fertile farmland and mixed forests, but in the southwest these give way to marshlands, sandy soil and pine forests. In the south and on the island of Corsica, you can walk through groves of olive trees and dry scrubland, known as *maquis*. Here, the air is scented with wildflowers and herbs.

Above the snow line

More than half of France is over 650 feet high. To the east, the country is separated from Switzerland and Italy by the Alps, a series of mountain ranges with the highest peaks in Europe. The tallest is Mont Blanc, at 15,771 feet. Its shining glaciers tower above the town of Chamonix. The higher Alpine peaks are snow covered all year and offer excellent skiing.

From the Alps the land gradually descends northward, through the Jura Mountains and the thickly wooded slopes of the Vosges toward the hills of the Ardennes. In the southwest, dividing France from Spain, are the rugged, snowy peaks of the Pyrenees.

In southwest France the sharp, rocky peaks of the Pyrenees contrast with the gentle foothills.

Old volcanoes

Between the Alps and the Pyrenees, the land rises to a height of over 6,500 feet above sea level. This is the Massif Central, formed from the remains of much older mountains that were once volcanoes. It includes a flattened region known as the Causses. This limestone plateau is pitted with huge caves, potholes, gullies and hot springs. Until recently the steep cliffs and gorges of the Massif cut it off from the rest of France.

Le Puy-en-Velay

In the Massif Central there are many outcrops of ancient volcanic rock. The pillar at Le Puy, shown below, was once a "plug" of lava inside a volcano. Over millions of years, the surrounding rock was worn away. About 900 years ago a church was built on top.

Chamois enjoy the mountain snows in winter.

Wildlife survival

The high mountain slopes of France are mainly undisturbed. Golden eagles wheel high in the sky. Small numbers of brown bears still survive in remote parts of the Pyrenees. Burrowing ground squirrels, called marmots, and small chamois antelopes may be seen.

The ibex, a wild goat, was nearly hunted to extinction but is now protected, as are Europe's only vultures. Unfortunately, wildlife is increasingly threatened by human activity. Habitats are being destroyed in order to make ski runs, and birds are killed when they fly into overhead cables.

Around the coast

Northern France borders the English Channel. This is called La Manche (the sleeve) by the French. Much of French history was made by seafarers sailing from the Channel ports. The low cliffs and sandy beaches also attracted invaders. In 1945 the Allied troops, fighting to free France from German occupation, landed on the beaches of Normandy. Many people visit this coast to see the memorials and remains from World War II.

In Brittany ocean waves have cut steep, rugged cliffs from the highland rock. The most westerly point of France is the razor-sharp Pointe du Raz.

Mount-Saint-Michel

This tiny island lies off the Normandy coast. Its magnificent abbey dates back more than 700 years. The island can now be reached by a causeway but was once cut off by the sea at high tide.

Pines and dunes

The cliffs of northern Brittany give way to the long sandy beaches and pine forests of the Atlantic coast. The Bay of Biscay has frequent storms, and the powerful waves along this coast are popular with surfers.

This coastline is broken by the estuaries of several of France's major rivers — the Loire, the Charente and the Gironde. Around the Charente is the Marais (marsh), a large wetland area.

Below the Gironde the sand has been blown into gigantic sand dunes. The Dune du Pilat, near Arcachon, is the highest in Europe. It is 384 feet high. In the early 1800s the French emperor Napoléon Bonaparte ordered pine forests to be planted along the dunes. The trees' roots anchor the shifting sands.

The Dune du Pilat – a mountain of sand!

Summer vacations

The south coast, with its hot Mediterranean climate, is a favorite place for vacations. The French usually stop working for the whole month of August. Pine forests and cypress and olive groves provide shade for thousands of campsites. Camping is very popular. The whole household moves, often bringing the cat and houseplants along too! There are frequent bushfires because the climate is very dry.

On the coast many small fishing villages have grown into large, famous resorts such as Cannes and Saint-Tropez. Unfortunately, the clear, blue water of the Mediterranean is becoming polluted with industrial waste and sewage.

Monaco

On France's Mediterranean coast is the tiny independent state of Monaco. It has an area of only 481 acres. Ruled by the Grimaldi family, it is famous for the gambling casino at Monte Carlo.

National parks

Many areas of France are now being protected. Five large national parks have been created in remote regions. There are also some 20 "protected regions" in more populated areas.

The round-up of wild horses in the Camargue.

The Camargue

Where the Rhône River enters the Mediterranean Sea, it forms a large delta. This marshland, with an area of 216 square miles, is a protected region. It is a haven for wildlife, including flocks of flamingos. Most of France's rice is grown here, and large areas have been drained. The Camargue is famous for its herds of white horses and its bulls, which are reared for bullfights.

Across France — by boat

With over 400 rooms, the Loire valley château of Chambord is the largest in France.

France has many waterways. They are used both for transportation and for pleasure. A good network of rivers and canals makes it possible to cross France by boat from the English Channel to the Mediterranean Sea. This network is based on four major river systems flowing from the mountains.

The Garonne River

The Garonne River rises in the Pyrenees and forms a mountain torrent. It is joined by other fast-flowing rivers, the Tarn, the Lot and the Dordogne, which drain the Massif Central. Where the Garonne flows into the ocean, it forms the broad estuary known as the Gironde.

The peaceful Seine

The Seine River is the most gentle of the major rivers and is open to shipping.

It rises in central France and crosses the rolling plains of the Paris Basin. Flowing northward through the center of Paris, it reaches the English Channel between Le Havre and Honfleur. On the way it is joined by the rivers Oise, Marne and Yonne, which flow from the Ardennes, the Vosges and from Burgundy.

The Loire

The Loire, the longest river in France, is 620 miles long and rises in the Massif Central. The river and its tributaries are all very swift and prone to flooding. To protect the farmland, raised banks, or *levées*, have been constructed along many stretches of the Loire. In the Loire valley there are many famous *châteaux*, built by past French kings and nobles.

A canal aqueduct passes over the Garonne River.

Down the Rhône River

The mighty Rhône rises in the Swiss Alps. At Lyon, France's second-largest city, it joins up with the Saône River, which flows down from the Jura Mountains. From Lyon the Rhône has been made into a canal to provide a safe waterway for the great barges that carry the many industrial products of the Rhône valley. At the mouth of the Rhône lies the marshy delta of the Camargue and Marseille, France's largest port.

Canals and lakes

As France is such a large country, waterways have always been important for transportation. Canals were built to improve the river network and to prevent flooding. Canals now link the industrial city of Toulouse, over 95 miles from the sea, with Bordeaux on the Atlantic coast and with the Mediterranean port of Sète. Far to the north, the Marne-Rhine Canal carries freight from Germany to Paris.

The Rhône-Rhine Canal makes up one huge waterway, linking northern and southern Europe.

Other smaller canals are used for quiet vacations. In Poitiers, canals were dug in the 1600s to drain the Marais. Their banks hung with willows, these picturesque waterways are only visited in flat-bottomed boats called *plates*.

France has several large lakes. Hourtin, near Bordeaux, is the largest. There are numerous smaller lakes in this region. The sparkling waters of lakes Annecy and Bourget lie near the mountains of Haute–Savoie.

Sports in the water

Fishing is a favorite French pastime, and lakes also provide swimming, sailing and windsurfing. Some high mountain lakes, such as Lac d'Oule in the Pyrenees, can only be reached by chair lift or a long hike. Rivers are also used for canoeing and rafting.

Many fast rivers in France are ideal for white-water boating.

Energy and industry

France is one of Europe's leading industrial powers. Its factories need a good supply of energy. The many powerful rivers and waterfalls in the mountains are harnessed for hydroelectric power. France produces about 25 percent of its electricity in this way. The power of the sea is also used. A dam on the Rance River in Brittany was the first in the world to use the movement of the tides to generate electricity.

Some oil for fuel is found in the Landes region of the southwest, and natural gas is found near the Pyrenees.

Using the sun

France has also experimented with other ways of making electricity. At Odeillo in the Pyrenees, a giant solar power station uses hundreds of movable mirrors to concentrate the sun's heat. This generates power.

The hundreds of mirrors on this building at Odeillo reflect sunlight into a furnace. The heat is used to make electricity.

This nuclear power station at Chooz is one of the newest of the 57 in France.

Nuclear power

About 75 percent of France's electricity is supplied by nuclear power. France has the world's second-largest nuclear power system, with 57 reactors. It also has the world's largest nuclear reactor. Nuclear power is unpopular in many countries, due to fears about its long-term safety and the expense of building and closing down nuclear power stations. The French system has a good safety record so far. It produces more electricity than can be used in France, so some of it is sold to Britain, Italy, Germany and the Netherlands.

France at work

France has rich natural resources. Coal, iron ore, uranium, chalk and limestone for cement are mined. Chemical production has become a major industry, as have electronics, aircraft and vehicle manufacture. France is the world's fourth-largest producer of cars, with well-known makes such as Renault, Citroën and Peugeot-Talbot.

Today, well over half of all French people work in service industries, such as banking or tourism. In France, many more people still work on the land than in, say, Britain or Germany. Farming is the largest industry. Wheat, barley, corn, rice and many varieties of vegetables and fruit are grown. Apples and grapes are major crops. In the south flowers are grown for the perfume industry. Huge areas of forest are grown for timber. Cattle, sheep, pigs and goats are raised for dairy products, leather goods and wool. Large fishing fleets sail from ports in Brittany and the west.

French industrial worker

Bon appétit!

Bread comes in all sizes and shapes in France!

As the climate of France varies so much from the north to the south, a wide variety of produce can be grown. Eating is seen as very important, and French cooking is thought by many people to be the finest in the world.

Bread is eaten at every meal, although less is eaten now than in the past. The French like their bread very fresh; it is often bought twice a day. The most popular loaves are the long, crusty *baguette* (bread stick) and the large, round *pain de campagne* (country loaf). Bakeries, or *boulangeries,* also sell rich, buttery *croissants.*

Every region has its own specialties. Seafood is served around the coasts. In the west there are fine lobsters and oysters. *Bouillabaisse*, a tasty fish stew, is a Mediterranean favorite. Brittany is famous for its *crêpes*, or pancakes. In Normandy, apples are used to make a liqueur called *calvados* as well as fruit tarts.

In the east bacon is used in *quiche lorraine* and in meat *pâtés* cooked with herbs and spices. Almost every region has its own *pâté*, but the most famous, made from goose liver, is *pâté de foie gras.* This comes from Perigord, also known for its wild fungi, especially the rare truffle that grows underground.

Cheese can be made in factories or on farms.

French cheeses

The French boast that they can offer 365 different cheeses, one for every day of the year! There may well be even more. Many cheeses are sold only in the area in which they are made. Others, such as *Camembert*, are sold all over the world.

Cheeses are made from the milk of cows, sheep or goats. They vary in texture from hard cheese, such as the *Cantal* of the Auvergne, to soft cheeses such as *Brie*, from the lush dairy pastures of Normandy. Among the most pungent are the blue cheeses. These are made by adding natural molds with skewers during ripening. The most famous of these cheeses is *Roquefort*, which is ripened in cool, dark caves in the Massif Central. There are also creamy cheeses, usually made from goats' milk. They vary in flavor and strength and are often rolled in herbs, peppercorns — or even wood ash!

Fine wines

Wine has been made in France since Roman times. It has led the world in producing fine wines, from sparkling champagne and the light white wines of the Loire region and Alsace, to the fruity wines of Burgundy. The heavier red wines from the Bordeaux region are considered by many to be the best in the world.

Quality control

French wine is labeled to show its quality: **appellation contrôlée** — the very best, strictly controlled; **vin de pays** — wine from a single region; **vin de table** — often a mixture of wines, sometimes from other countries.

Grapes are harvested in September.

Keeping in touch

Communication between the separate regions of France has always been important. During the late 1700s Emperor Napoléon built a good network of roads, the *routes nationales*. In 1783, the Montgolfier brothers invented air travel, with the first hot-air balloon, and in 1794 Claude Chappé built a machine to signal messages. France has continued to be a world leader in the development of communications.

Aerospace

By the 1970s France, together with Britain, had built the world's fastest passenger plane, the supersonic *Concorde*. With other European partners, the French have also developed the safe and efficient Airbus.

France was a founder member of the European Space Agency. It built the *Ariane* rocket and the SPOT satellite for recording images of the earth's surface. It designed the *Hermes* space shuttle.

Autoroutes and Alps

France has improved its transport system. Paris is the center of the network, and highways, or *autoroutes*, radiate out from the ring road around Paris, the *Périphérique*. Highways are given special names such as the *Autoroute du Soleil* ("Sunshine Highway"). Most roads in France are free, but on highways, tolls are charged to pay for upkeep. Some roads climb up the sides of steep mountains or else go straight through them — by tunnel!

Unless there is a tunnel, mountain roads climb steeply and have hairpin bends.

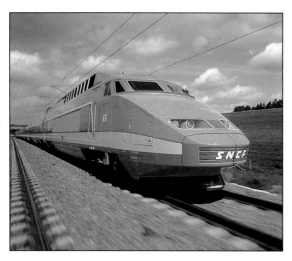

A TGV speeding through France.

Fast tracks

The railroads also radiate out from Paris. The network, one of the most efficient in the world, is run by the SNCF *(Société Nationale des Chemins de Fer Français)*. It has 21,750 miles of rail, with a third of it electrified. French trains include the record-breaking TGVs (*Trains Grande Vitesse*), which carry passengers from Paris to Lyon and other big cities at speeds of up to 180 mph.

Eurotunnel

Soon it will be possible to get from France to England without crossing water. French and British companies, working together, have built a 23 mile tunnel under the English Channel, from Sangatte near Calais to Shakespeare Cliffs at Dover. Special double-decker trains will be carrying passengers, vehicles and goods between France and England.

Telecommunications

In 1990 France became the first country to have a completely digital telephone system. *Numéris* allows voice, fax, photograph or computer data to be sent down a single line at the same time.

France Télécom has also created *Minitel*, a computer that offers access to what is possibly the world's largest data base. Over 5.6 million telephone users can use *Minitel*'s countrywide list of phone numbers for transportation and theater times, stores and services. *Minitel* terminals are also installed in banks and post offices.

Minitels being tested in the factory. Many French homes have one of these Minitels.

Where do people live?

France is less crowded than other countries in Western Europe. Although it is roughly twice the size of Britain, its population — 56 million — is about the same. It was not always like this. In 1800, France's population was nearly five times that of Britain.

Between 1870 and 1945 France was devastated by three wars with Germany. Many French people were killed and only 40 million were left. After World War II, French governments rewarded couples who had children with money and televisions. The state still pays families large sums in child benefits.

The population is spread very unevenly across the country. France has about 100 people per 0.4 square miles, but as few as 14 people per that area live in the mountains. Many people have left the countryside, and derelict houses are familiar sights in villages and small towns. People have moved into cities such as Lyon and Marseille, which both have populations of over a million.

The capital, Paris, has long been the heart of the country. It is the center of government, finance and business. More than 9 million people — 16 percent of the French population — live in the city and its suburbs.

As people move to cities, houses are left empty in old villages all over France.

The regions of France

In 1790 the French government divided the country into 96 *départements*, including Corsica. The aim was to run France more efficiently. Each *département* had a principal town, a number and a name, usually that of its main river. In 1955 France was also divided into 22 larger "metropolitan regions," with greater regional powers.

Spotting number plates

The number of each *département* is used for postal codes and for car registration. The last two numbers on a car's license plates make up the code of the *département* to which it belongs. For example, this car with **32** is from the *département* of Gers.

La Défense, a suburb of Paris.

New buildings

The traditional French way of life may still be seen in many old towns and villages. However, as towns expand, there are often large areas of new apartment buildings and housing developments. Although the French in towns have traditionally lived in apartments, there is a trend toward houses in new suburbs.

In the 1950s and 1960s the growing population and the damage done by World War II meant that many cities needed new housing. Some of the new homes were built according to bold designs. French architects are very inventive. Unfortunately, some of the suburban housing was of poor quality, and this now forms slums around cities such as Paris or Marseille.

Paris

The Eiffel Tower is the most famous landmark in Paris.

The Seine River winds through the center of Paris, and it is fun to see this beautiful city from a tourist boat, or *bateau-mouche*. At the heart of the city is an island called Île de la Cité, crowned by the cathedral of Notre Dame. Many nobles were imprisoned in the island's Palais de Justice during the French Revolution (1789–1799). The oldest bridge in Paris is called *Pont-Neuf* (New Bridge), although it is over 400 years old!

The Seine divides Paris into a "Right Bank" and a "Left Bank." Much of the city on the Right Bank was rebuilt to a new plan in the 1800s. There are wide boulevards such as the Champs Élysées, which runs from the Arc de Triomphe to the huge Place de la Concorde. Nearby are the Tuileries Gardens, next to the Louvre. This is the largest palace in the world, occupying over 0.6 miles of the Right Bank. On a hill beyond the Louvre is the white church of the Sacré Coeur and the artists' quarter of Montmartre.

On the Left Bank are the older, narrow streets of the student section, or Latin Quarter, and the Sorbonne University. Further down the river is the Eiffel Tower, on the Champs de Mars.

The Eiffel Tower

This is the best-known building in Paris. At 984 feet, it dominates the skyline. On a clear day you can see for 42 miles from the top. There are three viewing platforms that can be reached by elevator or by steps — all 1,652 of them! The tower was built in 1889 by Gustave Eiffel for the 100th anniversary of the French Revolution. A latticework of iron girders on four huge legs, it was the tallest building in the world until 1930.

Café life

A favorite pastime in Paris is to sit in a café and watch the world go by. There are hundreds of cafés to choose from, and you can sit indoors or at a table outside on the sidewalk. Cafés are popular meeting places for many people who live and work in Paris. Some cafés are in very *chic*, or smart, areas, such as the rue de Rivoli or Faubourg St. Honoré. In the past, many famous writers and artists met in such popular cafés as *Deux Magots* in Saint-Germain. Some artists still work in cafés in Montmartre, mostly painting portraits for the tourists.

Museums

The Louvre – This palace houses one of the world's largest museums. It is too big to see everything in one visit, but its most famous object is a painting by Leonardo da Vinci called *Mona Lisa*. The entrance is a modern glass pyramid in the main courtyard.

Musée d'Orsay – A good introduction to some of the world's most famous paintings, in a building that was once a railroad station.

Beaubourg – In the unusual Pompidou Center, this modern art museum also offers workshops and activities. You can ride up the outside of the center in a glass-tube escalator and watch jugglers and clowns perform below.

City of Science – A vast museum with robots and machines you can work, and a planetarium. Behind it is a movie theater in a huge mirrored dome, **La Géode.**

This exciting glass pyramid is built in the courtyard of the Louvre.

People and language

Who are the French? They are mostly descended from a number of ancient European peoples. These include a Celtic people, the Gauls, and various Germanic peoples such as the Burgundians and the Franks — who gave France its name. Normandy was originally settled by Vikings from Scandinavia. For the last 500 years, however, the French have formed a single people with their own language and way of life.

The borders of France also take in some non-French peoples. There are the Corsicans of the Mediterranean and the Catalans of the southwest. German-speaking people still live in Alsace, which has at times been part of Germany. Brittany has a long tradition of independence. Its people are descended from Celts, and many still speak Breton, which is a Celtic language.

The Basques

The Basques are a very ancient people. Their homeland is divided between Spain and France, where about 150,000 of them live. Traditionally farmers and sailors, they have a strong sense of identity. The Basque language, called *Euskara*, does not seem to be related to any other European language.

Fantastic lace headdresses are part of the national costume of Brittany.

Speaking French

The French language is spoken in France and in many other parts of the world too, from Africa to Southeast Asia. In 1635 the Académie française was set up to preserve the purity of the French language. However, in recent years many English words have become widely used.

In parts of France, such as Provence and Languedoc, you can hear dialects, or local versions, of French. Languedoc means the "language of *oc*." *Oc* was a word meaning "yes" — *oui* in modern French.

The new French

Not all French people are of European origin. In 1946 the French colonies of Guadeloupe, French Guiana, Martinique and Réunion became overseas *départements* of France. Recently many people from Algeria, Morocco, Vietnam and Iran have come to live in France itself.

An African using an Islamic book-store in Paris.

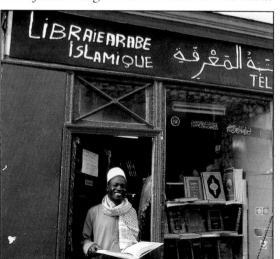

In the past, France has welcomed foreigners. Paris has been a center for artists and thinkers from many countries. Today, though, racists blame people of foreign descent for all kinds of problems.

Religious beliefs

Most French people are Christians of the Roman Catholic faith. However, there is no official religion. Traditionally public life has been dominated by Catholic priests. Each village, no matter how small, still has a Catholic church, and over 25 percent of the children attend Catholic schools rather than state schools. But many of France's 42 million Catholics do not go to church. Many French people of North African or Middle Eastern descent follow the Islamic faith.

In France, Roman Catholics have many feast days and processions, such as this one for St. Anne.

Leisure and the arts

During their free time, people in France enjoy eating out, visiting friends or taking part in sports. Sports are very popular in France. Older people often combine meeting their friends with playing the traditional game of *boules*. This form of bowling is often played outside a café. Special playing fields are found in the center of many towns and villages.

Children play volleyball, tennis and soccer at school. Swimming pools or sports halls at the *maison des jeunes* (youth clubs) are popular places to meet.

Although the sport of soccer has a big following in France, in the southwest rugby is very popular. Toulouse is the center of French rugby. France has a strong national team that competes successfully in international matches.

At the races

France is the home of car racing. World-class races include a 24-hour race at Le Mans and the Monaco Grand Prix, when cars race through the steep, winding streets of Monte Carlo. Horse racing too is popular. Elegant crowds gather at the Longchamps racecourse.

The Tour de France

This is the most important of all the races in France. Squeezed into three weeks in July, the punishing bicycle race covers a distance of 1,988 miles. It takes in some of the highest, steepest mountain passes in France. Hundreds of thousands of fans watch as the 200 cyclists rush by. Each day's leader wears a yellow jersey.

Summer and winter sports

Summer offers sailing, surfing, windsurfing and motorboat races. The mountains are ideal for hiking and climbing, and the winter's snow attracts skiers from all over Europe.

Barriers protect houses, as cars in the Le Mans motor race roar through the city.

Arts and crafts

Other popular pastimes include going to the theater, movies and art galleries. For centuries France has been famous for its artists and craft workers.

In the Middle Ages French nobles supported many artists. In the 1800s France became the world center of experimental art. Famous groups included the Cubists, with painters such as Georges Braque (1882–1963) and Spanish-born Pablo Picasso (1881–1973). There is still an interest in new art in France.

The Impressionists

Probably the most famous of all, this group of French painters was active from the 1870s into the 1900s. Artists such as Claude Monet, Édouard Manet and Auguste Renoir changed people's ideas on painting by showing "impressions" of light and images rather than exact copies of what they saw.

Monet painted this picture of London in 1904.

Words and music

Many of the finest poems of the Middle Ages were written in French, and in the 1600s there were the first French novels and the popular plays of Molière. France has produced many other brilliant writers such as Voltaire (1694–1778), Stendhal (1783–1842), Victor Hugo (1802–1885), Marcel Proust (1871–1922) and Simone de Beauvoir (1908–1986).

In music, France has produced great composers such as Georges Bizet (1838–1875) and Claude Debussy (1862–1918) as well as popular singers such as Edith Piaf (1915–1963). More recently Jean-Michel Jarre has become famous for his spectacular music and laser shows.

Jean-Michel Jarre's laser show in Houston, Texas

Motion pictures

In 1895 the French pioneered motion pictures when the Lumière brothers opened the first movie theater, in Paris. Since then French directors such as Jean Renoir and François Truffaut have become world famous. An international film festival is held each year at Cannes.

France in the past

People have been living in France for over 40,000 years. Les Eyzies in the Dordogne is at the heart of an area that has numerous prehistoric remains. The most famous of these are the caves of Lascaux, decorated with pictures over 10,000 years ago. In Brittany thousands of large stones called menhirs may still be seen. They date back about 5,000 years.

In later centuries fierce warriors called Celts spread across France. The Romans invaded their territory and named the region Gaul.

The Romans in Gaul

Gaul was completely conquered by 51 B.C. The Romans built cities and roads and brought in efficient government. Many remains survive from Roman times, including arenas, theaters and temples. The Pont du Gard in Provence was built to carry water to the city at Nîmes.

Eastern and northern invaders

From about A.D. 300 tribes from Germany began to invade Gaul. The Romans were driven out and Rome itself fell in A.D. 476. New kingdoms were set up by the invaders. The most successful was that of the Franks. By A.D. 800 the Frankish ruler Charlemagne had built up a large empire across Western Europe, setting up many Christian churches and schools.

During the 900s part of northern France was invaded in turn by Vikings. These "Normans" (from "Norsemen") were soon very powerful. In 1066 their leader, William, conquered England.

The Middle Ages

For much of the next 400 years the French and English fought over who owned France. In 1429 a young French girl called Joan of Arc (*Jeanne d'Arc*) rode into battle at the head of the French

There are 3,000 of these stones at Carnac, in Brittany. They were erected about 5,000 years ago.

army. She was later captured by the English, who burned her to death in 1431. She was only 19!

Religious wars

France was peaceful for a brief period, but then bitter wars broke out between Roman Catholics and Protestants. In 1572 over 20,000 Protestants, known as Huguenots, were massacred. Others fled abroad for safety. Many of them were skilled weavers. The Catholic church became more and more powerful.

The Golden Age

The 1600s and 1700s were France's Golden Age. Louis XIV made France the strongest power in Europe. France also conquered rich lands in the Americas, India and the Far East.

Louis XIV became known as *le Roi Soleil* — the "Sun King." His emblem, the sun, decorated his palaces. The most magnificent of these was Versailles, near Paris. This was the center of a glittering court.

Once, 5,000 people lived in the palace of Versailles.

Revolutionaries called for "Liberty or Death."

Revolution!

Although the nobles were very wealthy, ordinary people in France were desperately poor. There were unfair laws and taxes. On July 14, 1789, the French Revolution started, with an attack on the Bastille prison in Paris. This date is now a public holiday. During the revolution many thousands were sent to the guillotine to be executed. The king, Louis XVI, and his queen, Marie Antoinette, both had their heads cut off. France became a republic.

Napoléon Bonaparte

In 1799 the army, led by Napoléon Bonaparte, a young Corsican soldier, overthrew the French government. In 1804 Napoléon became emperor of France. Napoléon brought in many reforms and introduced a legal system still used in many parts of Europe today. He conquered much of Europe, but 400,000 French soldiers died during his disastrous invasion of Russia. Napoléon was finally defeated at Waterloo in 1815, by Britain and the German state of Prussia. He died in exile.

War and peace

During World War II Resistance fighters blew up trains to disrupt German communications.

France went through many changes during the 1800s. Royalists and republicans competed for power. In 1870–1871 France was beaten in a war with Prussia. The German soldiers besieged Paris, and the people in the city ended up eating rats! After this war the last king, Napoléon III, was removed from power, and France became a republic again.

Germany, now united as an empire, was France's main rival. Between 1914 and 1918 France, Britain and many other nations fought against Germany in World War I. The fighting was mainly in northern France, where the landscape was totally ruined. More than a million French soldiers died before Germany was defeated.

World War II

During the 1930s the German government was taken over by brutal racists called Nazis. In 1939 Nazi Germany started World War II, and from 1940 to 1944 France was once again occupied by German troops. It was a terrible period in which many French people, especially Jews, were killed.

Many brave French men and women fought secretly against the Nazis. They hid people the Germans wanted to capture and helped them to escape. They blew up German stores and arms.

Many of these acts by the Resistance movement were organized from Britain by French people who had already

Charles de Gaulle

escaped. The leader of this Free French Army was General Charles de Gaulle.

De Gaulle's France

From 1945–1946 General de Gaulle was President of France. Throughout the 1950s he was determined that France should become a successful nation again. He had strong ideas about the way to achieve that goal.

However, these were not easy years. There was fighting yet again, as French colonies demanded independence. France was defeated in Vietnam and fought a long, hard battle in Algeria. When it seemed that France would grant independence to Algeria, French colonists rebelled against their own government. De Gaulle was recalled to power in 1958, and Algeria did become independent.

France became wealthier, but in 1968

Paris was shaken by strikes and student riots. De Gaulle resigned, and he died in 1970. But his ideas were followed up by Presidents Georges Pompidou (1969–1974) and Valéry Giscard d'Estaing (1974–1981). A socialist president, François Mitterand, was elected in 1981 and again in 1988.

The European Parliament at Strasbourg

France in Europe

In 1957 France was one of the six countries that set up the European Economic Community, or EEC (now EC). Their aim was to allow free trade between member states. The EC now has 12 members and influences many aspects of life across Western Europe. France plays a leading part in the EC, and the European parliament is based at Strasbourg in northeastern France.

The years of peace have allowed France to develop as a major industrial country with a high standard of living and a key place in world affairs.

Fact file

Government

France has no king or queen. This kind of country is called a republic. France is a democratic country, which means that the people elect the rulers. The leader of the government, the president, is elected every seven years or less. The president chooses a prime minister and the other ministers in the government.

The French government is divided into two houses. The National Assembly has 577 deputies elected by the people for five-year terms. The Senate has 319 members elected by local councillors.

Political parties include the Gaullists (*Rassemblement pour la République*), the Centrists (*Union de la Démocratie Française*), the Socialists, the Communists and the National Front.

Flag

France's red, white and blue flag is called the *tricolore*. It dates from the French Revolution of 1789. The red and blue were the colors of the city of Paris and were placed over the white of the flag used by the French kings.

National anthem

"*Allons enfants de la Patrie*" (Come, children of our native land), France's stirring national anthem, the *Marseillaise*, was written in 1792. It was based on a song that was sung by revolutionary soldiers from Marseille.

Religion

France has no official religion, but approximately 75 percent of the population are members of the Roman Catholic church. Over 3 percent of the population are Muslim, while only 1.5 percent are Protestant.

Money

The unit of French currency is the franc. Each franc is divided into 100 centimes. The *Banque de France* issues coins for amounts from 5 centimes to 10 francs, and bank notes for amounts between 10 and 500 francs.

Education

Nursery education is available to French toddlers, and from six until 16 all children in France must go to school. At 11 they go to grammar schools (*lycées*), or secondary schools. Some children continue at *lycées* until they are 18. The final examination is called the *baccalauréat*.

Newspapers and television

France has many well-known newspapers. *France-Soir*, *Le Figaro* and *Le Monde* are based in Paris, but regional papers such as *Ouest-France* are also widely read.

There are two state-owned and five commercial television channels, plus satellite and cable. There are also many popular radio stations.

Some famous people

Jacques Cartier (1491–1557) and
Samuel Champlain (c.1567–1635)
explored North America

René Descartes (1596–1650) was a
philosopher and mathematician

Joseph (1740–1810) and **Jacques
Montgolfier** (1745–1799) invented
the hot-air balloon

Joseph Niepce (1765–1833) and **Louis
Daguerre** (1789–1851) pioneered
photography

André Ampère (1775–1836) was a
mathematician who studied electricity
and magnetism

Honoré de Balzac (1799–1850) was a
famous writer of novels

Louis Braille (1809–1852) invented a
system of raised dots to form letters for
the blind to read

Louis Pasteur (1822–1895) discovered
how to kill germs

Charles Blondin (1824–1897) crossed
Niagara Falls on a tightrope

Auguste Rodin (1840–1917) was one of
France's greatest sculptors

Sarah Bernhardt (1844–1923) was a
superb actress

Pierre (1859–1906) and **Marie Curie**
(1867–1934) discovered radium

Louis Blériot (1872–1936) made the
first flight across the English Channel

Coco Chanel (1883–1971) was a clothes
designer who made Paris the center of
world fashion, which it remains to
this day

Jacques Cousteau (1910–) is a famous
underwater explorer

Some key events in history

59 B.C.–A.D. **486**: occupied by the
Romans

768–814: Charlemagne made France the
center of an empire that included parts
of Italy and Germany

895: the start of Viking raids on France

1337–1453: England and France
fought a series of battles in the
Hundred Years' War

1431: Joan of Arc was burned to death
by the English

1562–1598: the religious wars between
Roman Catholics and Protestants

1643–1715: Louis XIV reigned

1789: the start of the French Revolution

1792: France became a republic

1799: the French army overthrew the
government, and Napoléon Bonaparte
became ruler

1804: Napoléon became emperor of
France

1815: French army led by Napoléon was
defeated at Waterloo

1870–1871: defeated by Prussia in the
Franco-Prussian War

1914–1918: at war with Germany in
World War I

1940: Germany invaded France in World
War II (1939–1945)

1944: France was freed from German
occupation

1954–1962: France at war with Algeria

1957: France joined the European
Community with five other European
countries

1945–1946, **1958–1969**: Charles de
Gaulle was president of France

Index